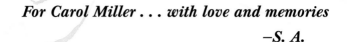

For Carol Miller . . . with love and memories

—S. A.

For W. R. S.

—D. S. M.

SIMON & SCHUSTER BOOKS FOR YOUNG READERS
An imprint of Simon & Schuster Children's Publishing Division
1230 Avenue of the Americas
New York, New York 10020
Text copyright © 1996 by Sue Alexander
Illustrations copyright © 1996 by David Scott Meier
All rights reserved including the right of reproduction in whole or in part in any form.
SIMON & SCHUSTER BOOKS FOR YOUNG READERS is a trademark of Simon & Schuster.
Book designed by Diane DePasque
The text of this book is set in 14/20 Baskerville
The illustrations were done in watercolor
Printed in Hong Kong by South China Printing Company (1988) Ltd.
10 9 8 7 6 5 4 3 2 1
Library of Congress Cataloging-in-Publication Data
Alexander, Sue, 1933–
What's Wrong Now, Millicent? / by Sue Alexander ; illustrated by David Scott Meier
    p.   cm.
Summary: Millicent complains about everything and even after her neighbor fixes things
for her, she is still not happy with the way things are.
[1. Hippopotamus–Fiction.   2. Neighborliness–Fiction.]   I. Meier, David Scott, ill.   II. Title.
PZ7.A3784We   1996   [E]–dc20   95-38291   CIP   AC
ISBN 0-689-80680-9

What's Wrong Now, Millicent?

by Sue Alexander

illustrated by David Scott Meier

Simon & Schuster Books for Young Readers

Ellsworth and Millicent were neighbors. They both lived
in comfortable cottages beside a rippling lake.

They both had big rose gardens and tree-shaded backyards.
They both had work they loved.
Most of the time they got along very well.

They both liked picnics and sunsets, raspberry ice cream and funny books, making castles in the sand and taking long walks in the hills.

But Millicent complained. About everything.

When they went wading in the lake Millicent complained, "The pebbles in this lake are stubbing all my toes!"

And when it rained she complained, "The rain on my roof sounds like a beating drum and it gives me a headache!"

And every time the wind blew she complained, "All the fluff from the dandelions in my yard blows into my ears!"

"I really like Millicent," Ellsworth thought. "If only she wouldn't complain quite so much."

The next day Millicent complained, "Drat! The thorns on these roses are scratching me all up!"

"I can fix that," Ellsworth said.

And he went into Millicent's garden and snipped every thorn off every rose.

"Now there are no more thorns," he said.

"No," Millicent said, "there aren't."

A few days later Millicent complained, "Something will have to
be done about the moon!"

"The moon?" Ellsworth said.

"Yes," said Millicent. "The moon shines so brightly that it
wakes me up at night."

"I can take care of that," Ellsworth said.

And he made shutters that fit Millicent's windows so tightly—not
even one small moonbeam could get through.

"Now the moon won't wake you up," he said.

"Those birds!" Millicent complained another day. "Something will have to be done about them. Their chirping disturbs my work!"

"I can fix that," Ellsworth said.
And he chased all the birds out of Millicent's trees.
"There. The birds are gone," he said.
"Yes," said Millicent "they are."
And she sighed.

Then Ellsworth picked all the dandelions so the wind would stop blowing their fluff into Millicent's ears. He put layers of cotton on Millicent's roof so the rain would stop sounding like a beating drum. And he took all the pebbles out of the lake so they would stop stubbing Millicent's toes.

There was nothing left for Millicent to complain about. But instead of being happy, she began to cry.

"What's wrong now, Millicent?" Ellsworth asked.

"It's the birds," Millicent cried. "I will miss hearing them!"

"Yes," Ellsworth agreed, "you will."

"And I miss seeing the moon at night!" Millicent sobbed.

"I thought you might," Ellsworth said.

"And my roses look forlorn without their thorns!" Millicent wailed.

"That's true," Ellsworth said, "they do."

Millicent stopped crying. She looked at her roses. She thought for a long time. Then she said, "You are a good friend, Ellsworth. Now let's put it all right again."

Together Millicent and Ellsworth put the pebbles back into the lake, took the layers of cotton off the roof, and planted dandelions (but just a few).

Then they spread bread crumbs to invite the birds back to the trees and made chinks in the shutters so that a moonbeam or two could get through.

A few days later Millicent said, "Drat! The roses have grown new thorns. I'm getting all scratched up!"

"That's nice," Ellsworth said.

Millicent smiled. "You're right, Ellsworth," she said. "It *is* nice."

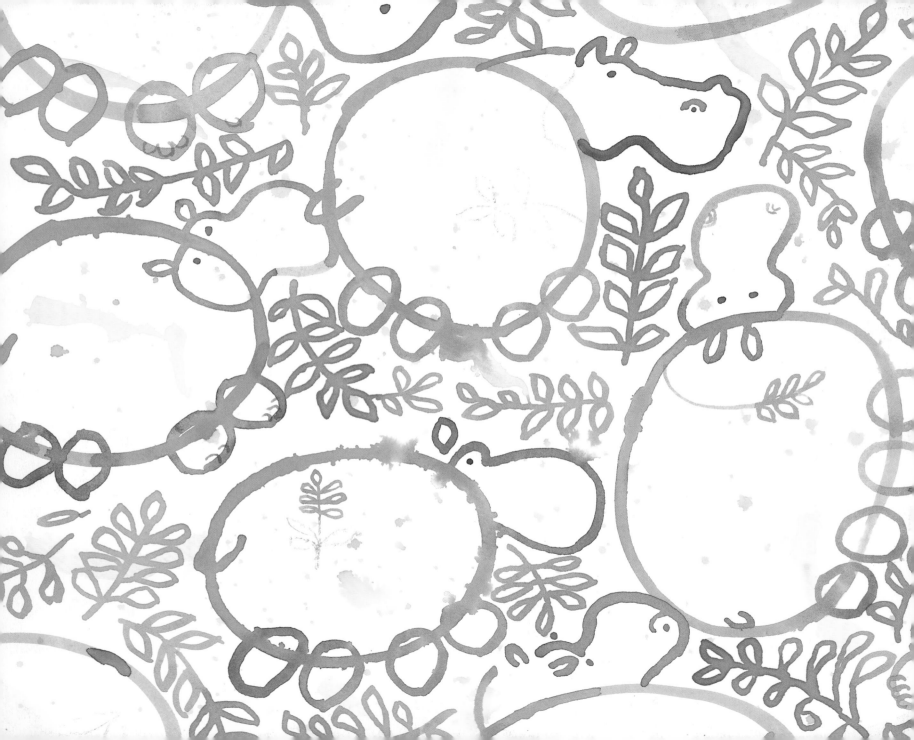